For my Mum and Dad. Always near — A.S.
For Elizabeth Nancy Georgina, my lovely Mum — L.M.

Too Small for My Big Bed was originally published in English in 2013
by Oxford University Press, Great Clarendon Street, Oxford OX2 6DP

First published in the United States in 2013 by Barron's Educational Series, Inc.

This edition is published by arrangement with Oxford University Press.

Text copyright © Amber Stewart 2013
Illustrations copyright © Layn Marlow 2013
The moral rights of the author and artist have been asserted

All inquiries should be addressed to:
Barron's Educational Series, Inc.
250 Wireless Boulevard
Hauppauge, New York 11788
www.barronseduc.com

ISBN: 978-0-7641-6587-0

Library of Congress Control Number: 2012947606

Date of Manufacture: December 2012
Manufactured by: Leo Paper Products, Heshan City, Guandong, China

Printed in China
9 8 7 6 5 4 3 2 1

Too Small for my Big Bed

AMBER STEWART   LAYN MARLOW

BARRON'S

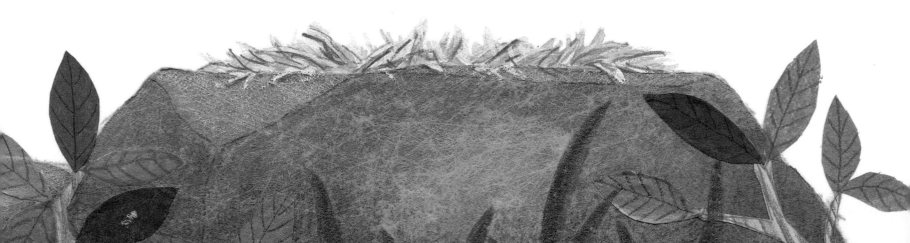

As Mommy kissed Piper
goodnight, she said to him,
"If you wake in the night, don't
come straight into Mommy's bed.

Try counting to more than ten.
Maybe that will help you fall
back to sleep in your own bed."

When *Piper did* wake in the night,
he tried counting . . .

1 2 3 4 5 6 7 8 9 10 . . .

10 and a bit . . .

10 and a bit more . . .

10 and a big bit more.

But he was still awake. And a wide-awake Piper didn't want to be alone in the deep, dark night. "I counted to more than ten," he whispered as he snuggled in beside his mommy.

"What a clever little cub you are,"
she sighed.

But Piper was already fast asleep
—spread out like a small star.

In the morning, Mommy took Piper
to the Golden Grasslands.

Piper pounced and jumped until he needed
to stop for a rest. "Today, I jumped higher
than ever!" he said happily.

"I know," smiled Mommy. "I've been watching. You jumped so high, and you did it all by yourself."
"All by myself!" laughed Piper.

But that night Piper still didn't want
to be all by himself in the deep dark.

The next day, Mommy took Piper climbing
along Red Rock Ridge.

Piper bounded easily to the top. "Mommy!" he called.
"Look at me. I'm going to be the king of the castle!"

"I know!" smiled Mommy.
"I'm watching . . .

You've climbed so far, and you've done it all by yourself."

"All by myself!" laughed Piper.

"Tonight, Piper," said Mommy, as they padded homeward, "if you wake in the night, try thinking about how high you jumped and how far you climbed—all by yourself. Then perhaps staying in your own bed—all by yourself—will seem easier."

Piper didn't look sure. "In the deep, dark night,"
he whispered, "my bed feels too big."
"It's not as big as my bed," said Mommy gently.
"But when I climb into your bed, Mommy," said Piper,
"you are near, to take away the bigness."

Mommy and Piper stopped at their favorite pond.

While they drank, Mommy asked, "How do you know I am near now, my clever little cub?"

"I can see your face wobbling in the water," said Piper.

"If you keep your eyes closed, and I am quieter
than the smallest cricket," asked Mommy,
"then how do you know I am near?"

Piper thought, and waited, and sniffed the air.
"I can just feel you, Mommy," he smiled.
"I can feel you are near."

"I'll never be far away," she said,
as they lay in the evening sun.

"Mommies never are."

When Piper woke that night, he looked into the
deep dark and . . .

though he couldn't see his mommy,

he could feel the cool night air
spreading her love around him.

And he knew that she was near.

So Piper snuggled down
further in his own bed,
and started counting to
more than ten.

But he only managed to
count as far as 1 2 3 before
he was fast asleep . . .

right through till morning.

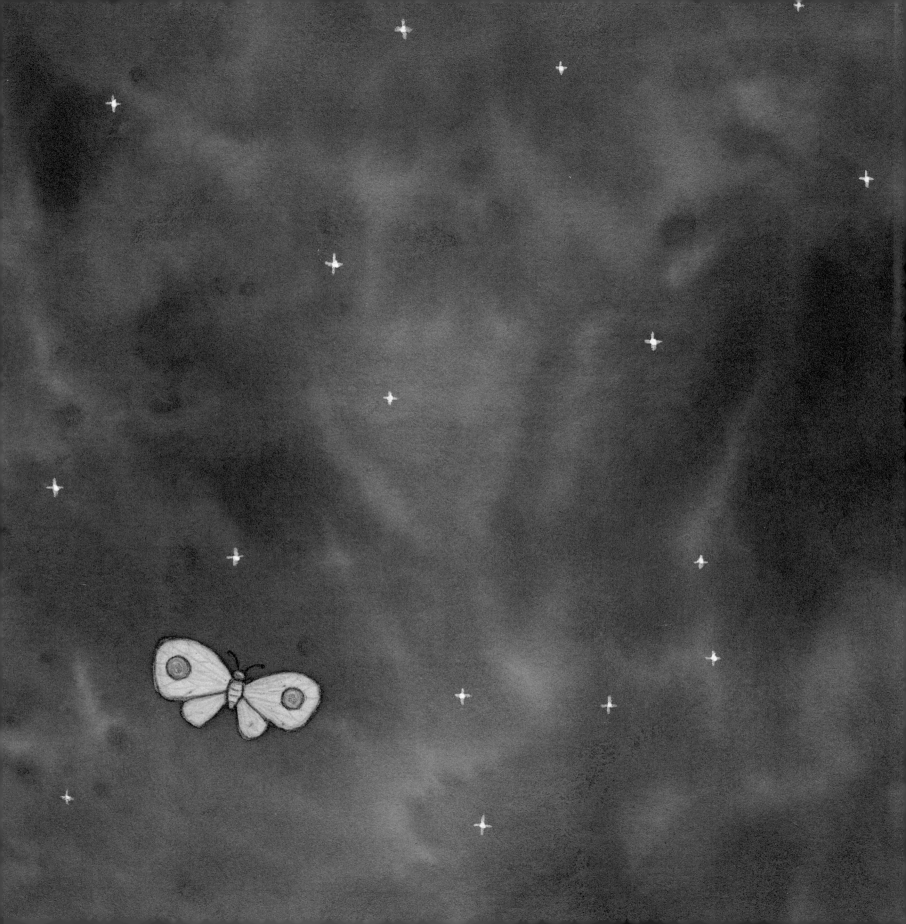